The F

Written by Jill Eggleton
Illustrated by Philip Webb

Rigby

Goat sat on the rock.
"I am the boss of this rock.
Look at my horns!" he said.

Fox sat down next to Goat.
"No one is the boss
of this rock," he said.

3

Goat was mad.
He put down his head and. . .

. . .**Poof!** Fox fell off the rock.

Goat laughed and laughed.
"Who is the boss?" he said.

Fox looked at Goat's horns.
"You are the boss," he said.

Rabbit came up to the rock.
He sat down next to Goat.

"Go away!" said Goat.

"I don't want to," said Rabbit.

"Look at my horns!" said Goat.
"I am the boss of this rock."

"No, you are not," said Rabbit.

Goat was mad. **Poof!**
Up, up, up went Rabbit. . .

. . .and down, down, down
came Rabbit.

Goat laughed and laughed.
"Who is the boss?" he said.

Rabbit looked at Goat's horns.
"You are the boss," he said.

Goat sat on the rock.
"Good! I am the boss," he said.

Bee sat down next to Goat.
"You are not the boss," said Bee.

"Yes, I am," said Goat.
"Look at my horns!
You haven't got horns like me."

Bee laughed and laughed.
He showed Goat his stinger!

"**Yeowww!**" said Goat.
"I don't like looking at that.
Please put it away!"

"Who is the boss
of this rock?"
said Bee.

Goat looked at Bee's stinger.
"You are the boss," he said.

"No," said Bee.
"I am not the boss,
and you are not the boss.
This rock is for us all."

A Flow Diagram

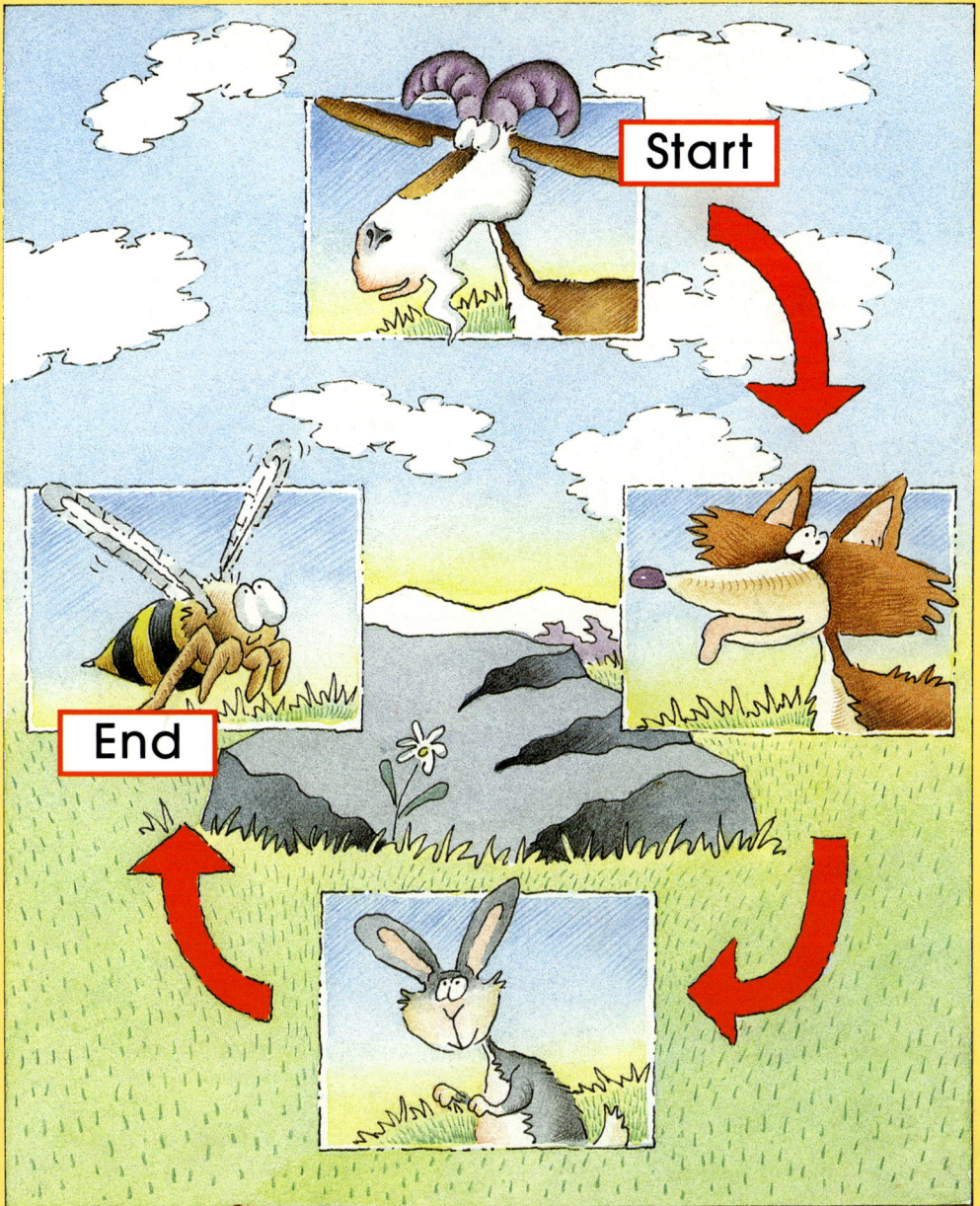

Start

End

15

Guide Notes

Title: The Rock Boss
Stage: Early (3) – Blue

Genre: Fiction
Approach: Guided Reading
Processes: Thinking Critically, Exploring Language, Processing Information
Written and Visual Focus: Flow Diagram
Word Count: 248

THINKING CRITICALLY
(sample questions)
- What do you think this story could be about?
- Focus on the title and discuss.
- Look at pages 2, 7, and 11. Why do you think Goat thought he was the boss of the rock?
- Why do you think all the animals wanted to be on the rock?
- Why do you think Goat thought there needed to be a boss?
- Look at pages 12 and 13. Why do you think Bee was not scared of Goat?
- What would you have done with Goat?

EXPLORING LANGUAGE

Terminology
Title, cover, illustrations, author, illustrator

Vocabulary
Interest words: boss, horns, stinger, rock
High-frequency words: who, want, haven't, us
Positional words: down, up, off, on

Print Conventions
Capital letter for sentence beginnings and names (**B**ee, **F**ox, **G**oat, **R**abbit), periods, commas, quotation marks, question marks, ellipsis, exclamation marks